WE GOT MY BROTHER
at the
ZOO

BY

JOHN and ANN HASSETT

Houghton Mifflin Company Boston 1993

For Katie and Elizabeth

Library of Congress Cataloging-in-Publication Data

Hassett, John.
    We got my brother at the zoo / John & Ann Hassett.
        p.   cm.
    Summary: Mary Margaret Morrison has a hard time adjusting to her
new baby brother and develops several outlandish stories about where
he really came from.
    ISBN 0-395-62429-0
    [1. Babies—Fiction.   2. Brothers and sisters—Fiction.]
I. Hassett, Ann (Ann M.)   II. Title.
PZ7.H2785We   1993   92-1681
[E]—dc20   CIP
                          AC

Printed in the United States of America

BVG   10   9   8   7   6   5   4   3   2   1

WE GOT MY
BROTHER
at the
ZOO

"Did you know we got my brother from the zoo?"

4

5

"He was in a cage full of wild beasts. He roared and screeched and chewed on bones, and he'd have bitten people for sure if he ever got loose. One day they were giving animals away, and we got stuck with him. Yup, it's true," said Mary Margaret Morrison.

"My brother's room used to be mine, but now I'm down the hall. My new room is far from things and dark as outer space, and I don't like it."

"Did you know we got my
brother from another planet?
He had two antennas on
his little green head, and he
wore shiny metal diapers, too.
He really did!"
said Mary Margaret Morrison.

"Me and my father, we liked to play games, and we used to quite a lot. Checkers was our favorite, and once I almost won. But that was in the good old days, before he got too busy."

"Did you know we got my brother from a bunch of monkeys? The monkeys live in a big tree in my back yard. Once, when my father was raking leaves, he spotted a baby at the tippety-top of the tree. My father caught him in a big monkey-catching net, and he became my brother. I'm not fooling!" said Mary Margaret Morrison.

"Me and my mother, we
liked tea parties the best.
She poured and I fixed
the cakes, and we said fancy
stuff like 'Please' and
'Thank you' and 'Oh dear,
such a mess!'
But we hardly have tea at
all anymore."

"Did you know we got my
brother from a band of
pirates? One day the pirates
stole my old toys and
buried them in my back yard.
I called the cops, but my
brother was too fast for 'em.
It really happened!"
said Mary Margaret Morrison.

19

"Grammy says my brother
has my father's ears and my
nose. *I* have my nose.
It's got two holes in it. But
it's mine, and I like it!"

"Did you know we got my
brother from the monsters
in my closet? One night
my father said, 'Enough!' and
he sent them all away. But
they forgot my brother, the
naughtiest one of all.
Yup, you bet,"
said Mary Margaret Morrison.

"But who knew he'd really do things that nice babies just never do. What if we have to send him right back to the place he really came from?"

"Did you know we got my
brother from the hospital?
My mother went there so
he could be born. He was in
a room full of wild babies.
They must give them all
away, 'cause we took him
home with us,"
said Mary Margaret Morrison.

THIS
SIDE
UP

"My brother's name is
Irwin Jr., and we are going
to keep him. He is almost
brand-new, so people
should never make up bad
stories about him . . .

"Or I'll sock them right in the nose!"

31

said Mary Margaret Morrison.